D~~ATE DUE~~

D1466492

GAYLORD   PRINTED IN U.S.A.

CALICO ILLUSTRATED CLASSICS

Bram Stoker's

DRACULA

ADAPTED BY: Karen Kelly
ILLUSTRATED BY: Ute Simon

magic
wagon

visit us at www.abdopublishing.com

Published by Magic Wagon, a division of the ABDO Group,
8000 West 78th Street, Edina, Minnesota 55439. Copyright
© 2011 by Abdo Consulting Group, Inc. International copyrights
reserved in all countries. All rights reserved. No part of this
book may be reproduced in any form without written permission
from the publisher.

Calico Chapter Books™ is a trademark and logo of Magic Wagon.

Printed in the United States of America, Melrose Park, Illinois.
102010
012011
 This book contains at least 10% recycled materials.

Original text by Bram Stoker
Adapted by Karen Kelly
Illustrated by Ute Simon
Edited by Stephanie Hedlund and Rochelle Baltzer
Cover and interior design by Abbey Fitzgerald

Library of Congress Cataloging-in-Publication Data

Kelly, Karen, 1962-
  Dracula / Bram Stoker ; adapted by Karen Kelly ; illustrated by Ute
Simon.
     p. cm. -- (Calico illustrated classics)
  ISBN 978-1-61641-101-5
  [1. Vampires--Fiction. 2. Horror stories.] I. Simon, Ute, ill. II. Stoker,
Bram, 1847-1912. Dracula. III. Title.
  PZ7.K29632Dr 2011
  [Fic]--dc22
                              2010030997

Table of Contents

CHAPTER 1

Jonathan Harker's Journal

May 3, Bistritz - I shall enter here some of my notes. They may refresh my memory when I talk over my travels with Mina.

In the population of Transylvania there are four distinct nationalities: Saxons, Wallachs, Magyars, and Szekelys. I am going among the Szekelys, who claim to be descended from Attila and the Huns.

I read that every known superstition in the world is gathered in the Carpathian Mountains. If so, my stay may be very interesting. (I must ask the Count all about them.)

It was on the dark side of twilight when we got to Bistritz, which is a very interesting old place. Count Dracula had directed me to go to the Golden Krone Hotel. To my great delight I found it to be thoroughly old-fashioned. When I got near the door, I faced a cheery-looking elderly woman in the usual peasant dress.

She bowed and said, "The Herr Englishman?"

"Yes," I said. "Jonathan Harker."

She smiled and gave some message to an elderly man who had followed her to the door. He went, but immediately returned with a letter for me.

My friend,

Welcome to the Carpathians. I am anxiously expecting you. At three tomorrow the coach will start for Bukovina. A place on it is kept for you. At the Borgo Pass my carriage will await you and bring you to me. I trust you will enjoy your stay in my beautiful land.

Your friend,
DRACULA

May 4 - Just before I was leaving, the old lady came to my room and said, "Must you go? Oh! Young Herr, must you go?"

She was in such an excited state she seemed to have lost her grip on what German she knew. She mixed it up with some other language I did not know at all. I told her I was engaged in important business. She asked, "Do you know what day it is?"

I answered that it was the fourth of May. She shook her head. "It is the eve of St. George's Day. Do you not know that tonight when the clock strikes midnight, all the evil things in the world will have full sway? Do you know where you are going?"

Finally, she begged me not to go. There was business to be done, and I could allow nothing to interfere with it. Taking a cross from around her neck, she offered it to me. It seemed ungracious to refuse an old lady.

I am writing up this part of the diary while I am waiting for the coach and the cross is still

around my neck. I am not feeling nearly as easy in my mind as usual. If this book should ever reach Mina before I do, let it bring my good-bye. Here comes the coach!

May 5, The Castle - When I got on the coach, I saw the driver talking with the lady. Every now and then they looked at me. Some of the people sitting on a bench outside the door came and listened. I could hear a lot of words repeated, strange words. I quietly got my dictionary from my bag and looked them up.

I must say they were not cheering to me. Among them were "Satan," "hell," "witch," and something that is either "werewolf" or "vampire." (I must ask the Count about these superstitions.)

When we started, the crowd round the door all made the sign of the cross and pointed two fingers towards me. With some difficulty I got a fellow passenger to tell me what they meant.

The fellow explained it was a charm against the evil eye. This was not very pleasant for me, but everyone seemed so kindhearted. Our driver cracked his big whip over his four small horses and we set off on our journey.

The road was rugged, but still we seemed to fly over it with a feverish haste. The only stop the driver would make was a moment's pause to light his lamps.

When it grew dark, there seemed to be some excitement among the passengers. They kept speaking to the driver, as though urging him to more speed. The crazy coach rocked on its leather springs and swayed like a boat tossed on a stormy sea.

We were nearing the Borgo Pass. We could now see the sandy road lying white before us. Among a chorus of screams from the peasants, a carriage came up behind and pulled up beside the coach.

The horses were driven by a tall man with a long, brown beard and a tall, black hat. I could only see the gleam of a pair of very bright eyes, which seemed red in the lamplight.

"Give me the Herr's luggage," said the driver. With great speed my bags were handed out and put into the carriage. Then off the coach swept on their way to Bukovina. A cloak was thrown over my shoulders and a rug across my knees.

"Mein Herr, my master the Count bade me take all care of you." The carriage went at a hard pace straight along.

Soon we were hemmed in by trees. It grew colder and fine, powdery snow began to fall. The baying of wolves sounded nearer and nearer, as though they were closing round on us from all sides.

A dreadful fear came upon me. I was afraid to speak or move. We kept on ascending. Then I realized the driver was pulling up the horses in the courtyard of a vast ruined castle.

Jonathan Harker's Journal

May 5 - When the carriage stopped, the driver jumped down and held out his hand to assist me. His hand seemed like a steel vice that could have crushed mine. He took out my luggage and put them on the ground beside me.

As I stood, the driver jumped again into his seat and shook the reins. Carriage and all disappeared down a dark opening.

I did not know what to do. There was no sign of bell or knocker on the great old door. Was this normal in the life of a lawyer's clerk sent to explain the purchase of a London estate to a foreigner?

There was the sound of rattling chains and the clanking of bolts drawn back. The great door swung back. A tall old man with a long, white mustache stood holding an antique silver lamp. He was dressed in black from head to toe.

The old man said in excellent English, "Welcome to my house! Enter freely and of your own will!" The instant I stepped over the threshold, his hand grasped mine with a strength that made me wince. His hand was also as cold as ice.

"Count Dracula?" I asked.

"I am Dracula. I bid you welcome, Mr. Harker." He insisted on carrying my luggage along the corridor and up a long winding stair.

At the end of another long corridor he threw open a heavy door. I rejoiced to see a well-lit room in which a table was spread for supper.

The Count halted to close the door behind us and then moved on to another room. Here was a bedroom that was well lit and warmed by a log fire. The Count left my luggage inside the room and withdrew from it.

"You will need to refresh yourself. When you are ready, come into the other room."

The light, the warmth, and the Count's welcome eased all my fears. After a hasty wash, I went into the other room.

My host, who stood by the stone fireplace, said, "Be seated and sup how you please. I trust you will excuse me that I do not join you. I have dined already."

He came forward and took off the cover of a dish, an excellent roast chicken. While I was eating, the Count asked me many questions about my journey.

I finished my supper and drew a chair up to the fire by the Count. I took the opportunity to observe him. His face was strong and his eyebrows massive. The mouth was cruel-looking with sharp teeth extending over his red lips. The rest of his skin was extraordinarily pale.

I looked toward the window and saw the first dim streak of the coming dawn. I heard the howling of many wolves. The Count's eyes gleamed, and he said, "Listen to them, the children of the night. What music they make!"

Then he rose. "But you must be tired. I have to be away till the afternoon, so sleep well and dream well!"

I am all in a sea of wonders. I think strange things that I dare not confess to my own soul. God keep me!

May 7 - I slept until late in the day. There was a card waiting for me on the table.

I have to be absent for a while. Do not wait for me. — D.

I enjoyed a hearty meal. When I finished, I looked about for something to read. There are odd shortages in the house compared to the wealth around me. The table service is gold and the curtains are of the most costly fabrics. But in none of the rooms is there a mirror. I have not yet seen a servant anywhere or heard a sound near the castle except the howling.

I found a sort of library. In it I found a vast number of English books, magazines, and newspapers. While I was looking at the books, the Count entered. We went thoroughly into the business of the purchase of the estate in London. Eventually, he excused himself, asking me to put all my papers together.

It was the better part of an hour when the Count returned. He said, "You must not work always. Come, your supper is ready." He took my arm and we went into the next room. I found an excellent supper ready.

The Count again excused himself from eating. After my supper the Count stayed with me, chatting and asking questions on every possible subject.

All at once we heard the crow of a cock. Count Dracula jumped to his feet. "There is the coming of morning again! How careless I am to let you stay up so long." With a courtly bow, he left me.

May 8 - There is something so strange about this place. I wish I were safe out of it.

I only slept a few hours when I went to bed. Feeling that I could not sleep any more, I got up. I had hung my shaving glass by the window and was just beginning to shave.

Suddenly I felt a hand on my shoulder and heard the Count's voice saying, "Good morning." I startled and cut myself slightly but did not notice it.

The man was close to me and I could see him over my shoulder. But there was no reflection of him in the mirror!

I saw blood was trickling down my chin. I turned to look for some bandage. When the Count saw my face, his eyes blazed and he made a grab at my throat. I drew away and his hand touched the string of beads that held the cross. It made an instant change in him.

"Take care how you cut yourself. It is more dangerous than you think in this country," he said. Then he seized the shaving glass. "This is the wretched thing that has done the mischief. Away with it!"

Opening the heavy window with one hand, he flung out the glass. Then he withdrew without a word.

After breakfast I did a little exploring. I found a room looking south. The view was magnificent. When I had seen the view, I explored further. Doors, doors, doors everywhere and all locked and bolted. In no place save from the windows is there an available exit.

The castle is a veritable prison and I am a prisoner!

Jonathan Harker's Journal

May 8 (Cont.) - My only plan will be to keep my knowledge and fears to myself and my eyes open. I heard the great door below shut and knew the Count had returned.

He did not come at once to the library, so I went cautiously to my room and found him making the bed. This confirmed that there are no servants in the house.

May 12 - Let me begin with the facts. Last evening the Count said to me, "Have you written to our friend Mr. Peter Hawkins or to any other?" I answered that I had not, as I had not seen any opportunity of sending letters to anybody.

"Then write now, my young friend," he said, laying a heavy hand on my shoulder. "Write to our friend and to any other and say you shall stay with me until a month from now."

"Do you wish me to stay so long?" I asked. My heart grew cold at the thought.

"I desire it much. I will take no refusal. I pray that you not discuss things other than business in your letters. It will please your friends to know that you are well." As he spoke he handed me three sheets of paper and three envelopes.

I understood well that I should be careful what I wrote, for he would read it. I determined to write only formal notes now and write fully to Mr. Hawkins and Mina in secret.

When I had written the letters, the Count took my two and placed them with his own. He stamped them carefully.

"I trust you will forgive me, but I have much work to do this evening. Let me warn you that you should not go to sleep in any other part of the castle. It is old and has many memories. There are bad dreams for those who sleep unwisely."

My only doubt was whether any dream could be more terrible than the horrible net of gloom and mystery that seems to be closing round me.

After a while, I went up the stone stair to where I could look out toward the south. I looked out over the beautiful expanse, bathed in soft yellow moonlight.

As I leaned from the window my eye was caught by something moving below me. I drew back behind the stonework and looked carefully out.

What I saw was the Count's head coming out from the window. The whole man slowly emerged from the window and began to crawl down the castle wall, face down. His cloak spread out around him like great wings. He moved downward with considerable speed, just as a lizard moves along a wall.

What manner of man is this? Or what manner of creature in the form of man? I feel the dread of this horrible place overpowering me.

May 15 - Once more I have seen the Count go out in his lizard fashion. I thought to use the opportunity to explore more than I had yet dared.

At last I found one door that was not locked. In the room, the furniture was more comfortable than any I had seen. A soft calm came over me.

Here I am, sitting at a little oak table. In old times a fair lady may have sat here to pen her poorly-spelled love letter. I am writing in shorthand in my diary.

Morning of May 16 - God preserve my sanity. When I finished writing in my diary and put my pen and book in my pocket, I felt sleepy. I determined not to return to the gloom-haunted rooms but to sleep there. I drew a couch out of its place so I could look at the lovely view. I suppose I must have fallen asleep but all that followed was startlingly real.

I was not alone. In the moonlight opposite me were three young women, ladies by their manners and dress. Two were dark and one was fair. All three had brilliant white teeth that shone like pearls against their ruby lips. They whispered together.

"Go on! You are the first. Yours is the right to begin," one said to the fair girl. The other added, "He is young and strong. There are kisses for us all."

The fair girl bent over me. I was afraid to raise my eyelids. I could feel the hard dents of two sharp teeth, pausing at my neck.

But the Count! Never did I imagine such fury. I saw his strong hand grasp the slender neck of the fair woman. With a fierce sweep of his arm he hurled the woman from him.

"How dare you touch him? This man belongs to me! When I am done with him, you shall kiss him at your will. Now go! I must awaken him for there is work to be done."

"Are we to have nothing tonight?" said one of them. She pointed to a bag he had thrown upon the floor. It moved as though there was some living thing in it. He nodded his head. As I looked, they disappeared with the bag.

Then the horror overcame me and I sank down in a faint.

CHAPTER 4

Jonathan Harker's Journal

May 16 (Cont.) - I awoke in my own bed. This room is now a sort of refuge, for nothing can be worse than those awful women who are waiting to suck my blood.

May 19 - Last night the Count asked me to write three letters. One saying that I should leave for home within a few days. One that I was starting the next morning from the time of the letter. And the third, that I had left the castle and arrived at Bistritz. I asked him which dates I should put on the letters.

He calculated a minute and said, "The first should be June 12, the second June 19, and the third June 29."

I now know the span of my life. God help me!

June 17 - This morning I heard a cracking of whips and pounding of horses' feet up the rocky path beyond the courtyard. I hurried to the window and saw two great wagons. I cried out to the men. They looked up at me and pointed but then turned away.

The wagons contained large square boxes with handles of thick rope. They were evidently empty, for the Slovaks easily handled them. They were all unloaded and packed in a great heap in one corner of the yard.

June 25 - Last night one of my dated letters went to post. Let me not think of it. Action! If only I could get into the Count's room. The door is always locked, no way for me.

Yes, there is a way. I have seen him crawl from his window. Why should I not go in by his window? I shall risk it. Good-bye, Mina, if I should fail.

Same day, later - I went while my courage was fresh and at once got outside on the narrow ledge that runs round the building. I took off my boots and made for the Count's window.

I raised up the sash and slid feetfirst in through the window. The room was empty! The only thing I found was a heap of gold in one corner, covered with dust.

At another corner of the room was a heavy door. It was open and led through a stone passage to a circular stairway that went steeply down. At the bottom was a dark passage, through which came a deathly odor.

I went through the passage and found myself in an old, ruined chapel. In two places there were steps leading down into vaults. In the third vault, I made a discovery.

In one of the many great boxes, lay the Count on a pile of newly dug earth! By the side of the box was its cover, pierced with holes here and there. I thought he might have the keys on him. But when I searched, I saw in the dead eyes such a look of hate that I fled from the place.

Reaching my own chamber, I threw myself panting upon my bed.

June 29 - Today is the date of my last letter. I was awakened by the Count, who looked at me grimly.

"Tomorrow, my friend, we must part. Tomorrow I shall not be here, but all shall be ready for your journey. My carriage will come for you and bear you to the Borgo Pass to meet the coach."

The last I saw of Count Dracula was him kissing his hand to me with a red light of triumph in his eyes. When I was in my room, I heard a whispering at my door. I went to it softly and listened. I heard the voice of the Count.

"Back to your own place! Have patience. Tomorrow night is yours!" There was a low ripple of laughter and in a rage I threw open the door. I saw the three terrible women licking their lips. As I appeared, they all joined in a horrible laugh and ran away.

June 30, morning - These may be the last words I ever write in this diary. While I wait, I can hear in the distance a gypsy song and the rolling of heavy wheels. As I write there is in the passage below a sound of many tramping feet. There is the sound of hammering. It is the box being nailed down.

The door is shut and the chain rattles. Hark! Down the rocky way the heavy wheels, cracking of whips, and chorus of the Szgany pass into the distance.

I am alone in the castle with those awful women. I shall try to scale the castle wall. I shall take some of the gold with me. I may find a way from this awful place.

Mina Murray's Journal

Letter, Lucy Westenra to Mina Murray

May 24

My dearest Mina,

It never rains, but it pours. I have never had a proposal till today and today I have had three. I feel sorry for two of the poor fellows.

Number one came just before lunch, Dr. John Seward. Handsome and well-off, he is only twenty-nine and has a lunatic asylum all under his care. I felt it my duty to tell him there was someone. He said he hoped I would be happy.

Number two came after lunch. He is such a nice fellow, an American from Texas. He took my hand and said ever so sweetly: "Miss Lucy, won't you hitch up alongside of me and let us go down the long road together, driving in double harness?"

I suppose there was something in my face because he then paused and said, "Is there anyone else you care for? If there is, I will be a very faithful friend."

I was able to look into Mr. Morris's brave eyes and tell him out straight. I need not tell you about number three, need I? I am very, very happy.

Your ever-loving,

Lucy

Mina Murray's Journal

July 24, Whitby - Lucy met me at the station, looking sweeter and more lovely than ever. We drove up to the house at the Crescent in which they have rooms. This is a lovely place.

Between the ruins of Whitby Abbey and the town there is another church with a big graveyard. People go and sit there all day long enjoying the view of the harbor.

Lucy and I sat there awhile. She told me all about Arthur Godalming and their coming marriage. That made me a little heartsick, for I haven't heard from Jonathan for a whole month.

July 26 - I am anxious. Yesterday dear Mr. Hawkins sent me a letter from Jonathan. I had written to him, asking if he had heard. He said the enclosed letter had just been received. It was only a line dated from Castle Dracula and says that he is just starting for home. This is not like Jonathan.

Lucy is well but has lately taken up her old habit of sleepwalking.

August 6 - This suspense is getting dreadful. And the fishermen say we are in for a storm. The sun is hidden in thick clouds, high over the harbor. The coastguard came along with his spyglass under his arm. He stopped to talk to me, but all the time he kept looking at a strange ship.

"She's a Russian by the look of her," he said. "But she's knocking about in the weirdest way. We'll hear more of her by this time tomorrow."

Cutting from the DailyGraph, August 8 (Pasted in Mina Murray's Journal)

One of the most sudden storms on record has just been experienced here with results both strange and unique. The searchlight discovered a schooner with all sails set, rushing at such speed toward the East Pier. The wind shifted and swept the schooner into the safety of the harbor. The searchlight followed her and a shudder ran through all who saw. Tied to the wheel was a corpse and no other form could be seen on the deck at all.

Strangest of all, the very instant the shore was touched, an immense dog sprang up on deck from below. It jumped onto the sand and disappeared in the darkness. It turns out the schooner is a Russian from Varna. She had only a small amount of cargo, a number of large wooden boxes filled with earth.

Mina Murray's Journal

August 10 - The funeral of the poor sea-captain today was most touching. I fear Lucy is of too sensitive a nature to go through the world without trouble. She will be dreaming of this tonight, I am sure. The whole jumble of things—the ship steered into port by a dead man, his being tied to the wheel with a cross and beads, the touching funeral, and the dog. They will all provide material for her dreams.

August 11, 3 a.m. - I am too distressed to sleep. I had fallen asleep but awoke with a horrible sense of fear upon me. The room was dark and I could not see Lucy's bed. I stole across and felt for her. The bed was empty.

I took a shawl and ran out. There was a bright full moon. I could see the ruins of the abbey coming into view. On our favorite seat the silver light of the moon struck a figure, snowy white. I flew up the steep steps to the abbey.

There was something, long and black, bending over the figure. I called in fright, "Lucy! Lucy!" Something raised a head and I could see a white face and red, gleaming eyes. I lost sight of her for a minute as I entered the churchyard. When I came in view again, Lucy was quite alone.

When I bent over her, I could see she was still asleep. I fastened the shawl at her throat with a big safety pin. I must have pricked her, for Lucy put her hand to her throat and moaned. We got home without meeting a soul and I tucked her into bed. I have locked the door and the key is tied to my wrist.

Same day, noon - I was sorry to notice that my clumsiness with the safety pin hurt Lucy. I must have pinched up a piece of loose skin and pierced it. There are two little red points like pinpricks. Lucy laughed and said she did not even feel it.

August 13 - Again I awoke in the night and found Lucy sitting up in bed, still asleep, and pointing to the window. I pulled aside the blind and looked out.

Between me and the moonlight flitted a great bat. It came and went in big, whirling circles. I suppose it was frightened at seeing me. It flitted away across the harbor toward the abbey. Lucy did not stir again all night.

August 17 - I have not had the heart to write. No news from Jonathan and Lucy seems to be growing weaker. I trust her feeling ill may not be from that unlucky prick of the safety pin.

I looked at her throat while she lay asleep and the wounds seem not to have healed. They are still open and larger than before. Unless they heal within a day or two, I shall insist on the doctor seeing about them.

August 19 - Joy, joy, joy! At last, news of Jonathan. The dear fellow has been ill. That is why he did not write. I am to leave in the morning and go to Jonathan to nurse him and bring him home. Mr. Harkins says it would not be a bad thing if we were to be married out there.

CHAPTER 6

Lucy Westenra's Diary

Letter, Mina Harker to Lucy Westenra

Buda-Pesth, August 24

My dearest Lucy,

I found my dear one, oh, so thin and pale and weak. He has had some terrible shock. Sister Agatha tells me he raved of dreadful things while he was off his head.

When he last awoke, he asked me for his coat for he wanted to get something from its pocket. He put his hand over his notebook and spoke very solemnly to me.

"Here is the book. Take it and keep it. Read it if you will, but never let me know."

I took the book and wrapped it up in white paper, tying a bit of pale blue ribbon around it. I told him I would never open it unless it were for his own dear sake or the sake of some important duty.

Good-bye, my dear. I must stop, for Jonathan is waking and I must attend my husband.

Your ever-loving,
Mina Harker

Lucy Westenra's Diary
August 24, Hillingham - I must imitate Mina and keep writing things down. Last night I seemed to be dreaming again, just as I was at Whitby.

August 25 - Another bad night. There was a sort of flapping at the window. But I suppose I must have then fallen asleep. More bad dreams. This morning I am horribly weak and my throat pains me.

Letter, Arthur Holmwood to Dr. Seward
August 31
Dear Jack,

I want you to do me a favor. Lucy is ill and is getting worse every day. I told her I should ask you to see her and she consented. It will be a painful task for you, but it is for her sake. You

are to come to lunch at Hillingham tomorrow, two o'clock. Do not fail!
Arthur

Telegram, Arthur Holmwood to Dr. Seward

September 1 - Am summoned to see my father, who is doing worse. Write me.

Letters from Dr. Seward to Arthur Holmwood

September 2

My dear old fellow,

With regard to Miss Westenra's health, there is not any sickness that I know of. At the same time, I am not satisfied with her appearance. I am in doubt and so have done the best thing I know.

I have written to my old friend and master, Professor Van Helsing, from Amsterdam. He knows as much about mysterious diseases as anyone in the world. I have asked him to come at once.

September 3

My dear Art,

Van Helsing has come and gone. He made a very careful examination of the patient. I fear he is much concerned but says he must think. I shall keep a stern watch.

Telegram, Seward to Van Helsing

September 6 - Terrible change for the worse. Come at once.

Dr. Seward's Diary

September 7 - I was horrified when I saw her today. She was ghastly pale and her breathing was painful to see or hear. Van Helsing's face grew set as marble. Lucy lay motionless and did not seem to have the strength to speak. Van Helsing motioned to me and we went gently out of the room.

"There is no time to be lost," he said. "She will die from lack of blood. There must be a transfer of blood at once. Is it you or me?"

"I am younger and stronger, Professor. It must be me."

"Then get ready, I will bring up my bag." When we reached the downstairs hall the maid had just opened the door. Arthur was stepping in. He rushed up to me.

"Jack, I was so anxious. What can I do?" asked Arthur.

The professor explained, "Young miss is bad, very bad. She wants blood and blood she must have or die. We are about to do a transfer of blood. John was to give his blood but now you are here. You are more good than us."

Van Helsing performed the transfer with swiftness. As it went on life seemed to come back into Lucy's cheeks. When it was all over, I could see how much Arthur was weakened. I dressed the wound and took his arm to bring him away.

When Arthur had gone, I went back to the room. By Lucy's bedside sat Van Helsing, looking at her intently. The professor stood up.

"I must go back to Amsterdam tonight," he said. "There are books and things there that I want. You must remain here all night."

Lucy Westenra's Diary
September 9 - I feel so happy tonight. Somehow Arthur feels very, very close to me. How I slept with that dear Dr. Seward watching me. Thank everybody for being so good to me! Thank God!

Dr. Seward's Diary
September 10 - I was aware of the Professor's hand on my head and started awake all in a second.

"How is our patient?" Together we went into the room. I raised the blind, and the morning sunlight flooded the room. I heard the professor's low hiss.

There on the bed lay poor Lucy, more horribly white than ever. Together we rubbed palm and wrist and heart.

After a few moments he said, "It is not too late. I have to call on you this time, friend John."

Without a moment's delay, we began the operation. It was with a feeling of personal pride that I could see a faint tinge of color steal back into the white lips and cheeks.

September 11 - This afternoon I went over to Hillingham. Found Van Helsing in excellent spirits and Lucy much better. Shortly after I arrived, a big parcel came for the professor. He opened it and showed a great bundle of white flowers.

"These are for you, Miss Lucy," he said.

"For me? Oh, Dr. Van Helsing!"

"Yes, my dear, but not for you to play with. These are medicines." While he was speaking, Lucy had been examining the flowers and smelling them. She threw them down.

"Oh, Professor, I believe you are only putting up a joke on me. Why these flowers are only common garlic," Lucy exclaimed.

"Come with me, friend John." We went into the room, taking the flowers with us. First, he secured the windows. Next, he took a handful of the flowers and rubbed them all over the frames, the doorjambs, and around the fireplace. He began to make a wreath which Lucy was to wear round her neck.

When Lucy was in bed, he came and fixed the wreath of garlic around her neck. The last words he said to her were, "Take care you do not disturb it. And even if the room feels uncomfortable, do not tonight open the window or the door."

Dr. Seward's Diary

Lucy Westenra's Diary

September 11 - I never liked garlic before, but tonight it is delightful! There is peace in its smell. I feel sleep coming already.

Dr. Seward's Diary

September 12 - Van Helsing and I arrived at Hillingham at eight o'clock. When we entered, we met Mrs. Westenra coming out of the morning room. She greeted us warmly and said, "You will be glad to know that Lucy is better. The dear child is still asleep."

The professor rubbed his hand together. "Aha! My treatment is working."

"You must not take all the credit yourself, doctor. Lucy's state this morning is due in part to me. The room was so awfully stuffy. There were a lot of those horrible flowers everywhere. I feared the heavy odor would be too much for her so I took them all away and opened the window."

When she moved off to have breakfast, I saw the professor's face turn gray. "Come, we must act." Together we went up to Lucy's room.

This time Van Helsing did not start as he looked on the poor face with the same awful paleness as before.

"As I expected," he murmured. I had begun to take off my coat, but he stopped me with a warning hand. "No! Today you must operate. I shall provide."

Again the operation, again the return of some color and of regular breathing. After a rest, Van Helsing took the opportunity to tell Mrs. Westenra that she must not remove anything from Lucy's room without consulting him.

He took over the care of the case himself, saying he would watch this night and the next. He will send word to me when to come.

After another hour, Lucy waked from her sleep, fresh and bright. She is seemingly not much the worse for her terrible ordeal.

Lucy Westenra's Diary

September 17 - Four days and nights of peace. I am getting so strong again that I hardly know myself. It is as if I had passed through some long nightmare and awakened to beautiful sunshine.

I found Dr. Van Helsing asleep twice when I awoke. But I did not fear to go to sleep again, although the tree limbs or bats flapped most angrily against the window.

Telegram, Van Helsing, Antwerp, to Seward, Carfax (Sent to wrong county, delivered late by twenty-two hours)

September 17 - Do not fail to be at Hillingham tonight. Very important. Shall be with you as soon as possible.

Memo left by Lucy Westenra

September 17 - I feel I am dying of weakness, but it must be done if I die in the doing.

Mother came in and sat by me. The flapping came to the window again. She was startled and cried out, "What is that?" I tried to calm her.

After a while there was a low howl out in the shrubbery. There was a crash at the window and broken glass was hurled on the floor. In the opening of the broken panes there was the head of a giant gray wolf.

Mother cried out and reached for something to support her. She clutched the wreath of flowers Dr. Van Helsing put round my neck and tore it away from me.

There was a horrible gurgling in her throat. Then she fell over as if struck by lightning. I tried to stir but there was some spell on me and dear mother's poor body weighed me down. I remembered no more for a while. Good-bye, dear Arthur, if I should not survive this night.

Dr. Seward's Diary

September 18 - After receiving the telegram, I drove at once to Hillingham and arrived early. I met Van Helsing running up the avenue. With white faces and trembling hands we entered Lucy's room.

On the bed lay two women, Lucy and her mother. Without a word the professor bent over the bed.

"It is not yet too late! Quick!" We took Lucy into another room. "We must consult as to what is to be done," he said as we descended the stairs after settling our patient. In the hall he opened the dining room door and we passed in.

"What are we to do now? We need another transfer of blood. What are we to do for someone to open his vein for her?"

"What's the matter with me anyhow?" The voice came from the sofa across the room and brought relief to my heart.

"Quincey Morris! What brought you here?" I cried and rushed toward him.

"I guess Art is the cause." He handed me a telegram:

"Have not heard from Seward for three days and am terribly anxious. Cannot leave. Send me word how Lucy is. Do not delay. Holmwood."

"You have only to tell me what to do."

Van Helsing strode forward and shook his hand. Once more we went through that horrid operation. Her body did not respond to the treatment as well as the other times. But her heart and lungs improved. I fear the shock has been too great. The poor child cannot rally.

September 20 - Only habit can let me make an entry tonight. I am too miserable.

At six o'clock Van Helsing came to relieve me. Arthur had fallen into a doze. Van Helsing removed the flowers and lifted the silk handkerchief from Lucy's throat. I could hear his, "Mein Gott!" I bent over and looked, too.

The wounds on the throat had disappeared.

Van Helsing said, "She is dying. It will not be long now. Wake that poor boy and let him come see the last. We have promised him."

When we came into the room Lucy opened her eyes and whispered softly, "Arthur! Oh, my love. I am so glad you have come!"

He was stooping to kiss her, when Van Helsing motioned him back.

"No, not yet!" he whispered. "Hold her hand."

Her eyes closed and she breathed heavily. Then she took Van Helsing's hand and kissed it. "My true friend, and his! Oh, guard him and give me peace!"

"I swear it," he said. Then he said to Arthur, "Come and kiss her on the forehead, and only once." And Lucy's breath became shallow and all at once ceased.

"She is dead," said Van Helsing. I took Arthur by the arm and led him away to the drawing room. I went back to the room.

I stood beside Van Helsing and said, "Poor girl, there is peace for her at last. It is the end!"

He turned to me. "Not so, alas! It is only the beginning."

When I asked him what he meant, he only shook his head and answered, "We can do nothing as yet. Wait and see."

Mina Harker's Journal

September 22 - In the train to Exeter. Jonathan sleeping. It seems only yesterday the last entry was made. And yet, how much has happened.

Now married to Jonathan. Jonathan an attorney, rich and master of his business. Mr. Hawkins dead and buried. Jonathan now with another attack that may harm him.

We came back to town quietly and walked down Piccadilly. I was looking at a beautiful girl in a big hat sitting in a carriage, when Jonathan clutched my arm.

I turned to him and asked him what disturbed him. His eyes seemed to be bulging out as he gazed at a tall man with a beaky nose and black mustache. The man's big, white teeth were pointed like an animal.

The dark man kept his eyes fixed on the woman in the carriage. When the carriage moved up Piccadilly, he followed in the same direction.

Jonathan said to himself, "I believe it is the Count, but he has grown young. Oh, if it be so! If only I knew!" I drew him away quietly.

I must somehow learn the facts of his journey abroad. The time is come, I fear, when I must open that parcel and know what is written.

Later - A sad homecoming in every way. The house empty of the dear soul who was so good to us. Jonathan still pale and dizzy. And now a telegram from Van Helsing, whoever he may be.

"You will be grieved to hear that Mrs. Westenra died five days ago and Lucy died the day before yesterday. They were both buried today."

What a wealth of sorrow in a few words. Poor Arthur, to have lost such sweetness out of his life.

The Westminster Gazette

The Hampstead Horror

We have just received information that another missing child was discovered in the morning under a bush of Hampstead Heath. It has the same tiny wound in the throat as has been noticed in other cases. It, too, had the common story to tell of being lured away by the "beautiful lady."

Mina Harker's Journal

September 23 - My household work is done. I shall take Jonathan's foreign journal, lock myself up in my room, and read it.

September 24 - That terrible record of Jonathan's upset me so. How he must have suffered, whether it be true or only imagination. I wonder if there is any truth in it at all. I shall get my typewriter this very hour and begin transcribing.

Letter, Van Helsing to Mrs. Harker

September 24

Dear Madam,

By the power of Lord Godalming I am able to read Miss Lucy Westenra's letters and papers. In them I find some letters from you, which show how great friends you were. Madam Mina, I implore you, help me. May it be that I see you? I am friend of Dr. John Seward and Lord Godalming.

Van Helsing

Telegram, Mrs. Harker to Van Helsing

September 25 - Come today by quarter-past ten train, if you can catch it. Can see you any time you call. Wilhelmina Harker

Mina Harker's Journal

September 25 - He has come and gone. Oh, what a strange meeting! Can it be possible? If I had not read Jonathan's journal first, I should never have accepted even the possibility. Poor, dear Jonathan! But it may be a help to him to know for certain that his eyes and ears did not deceive him and it is all true.

Dr. Seward's Diary

September 26 - Truly there is no such thing as final. Van Helsing came back from Exeter today. He almost bounded into the room and thrust last night's *Westminster Gazette* into my hand.

"What do you think of that?" he asked. He pointed out a paragraph about children being lured away at Hampstead. It did not mean much to me until I reached a part that described small puncture wounds on their throats. I looked up.

"Well?" he said.

"It is like poor Lucy's."

"And what do you make of it?"

"Simply that whatever it was that injured her has injured them."

"You think then that those so small holes in the children's throats were made by the same that made the hole in Miss Lucy?"

"I suppose so."

He stood up and said solemnly, "Then you would be wrong. But alas, no. It is worse, far worse."

"Professor Van Helsing, what do you mean?" I cried.

He threw himself into a chair, and covered his face with his hands. "They were made by Miss Lucy!"

Dr. Seward's Diary

September 26 (Cont.) - I hit the table hard and rose up as I said to him, "Dr. Van Helsing, are you mad?" He raised his head and the tenderness of his face calmed me.

"Madness would be easy to bear compared to truth like this," he said. "Even yet, I do not expect you to believe. Tonight I go to prove it. Dare you come with me?" He took a key from his pocket and held it up.

"Tonight we spend the night in the churchyard where Lucy lies. This is the key that locks the tomb." I plucked up what heart I could and said we had better hurry.

At last we reached the wall of the churchyard, which we climbed over. We found the Westenra tomb. The professor took the key, opened the creaky door, and motioned for me to go before him. My companion followed me closely and drew the door closed. He drew a matchbox and a candle from his bag and made a light.

Holding the candle so he could read the coffin plates, he found Lucy's coffin. He began taking out the screws and finally lifted off the lid. I drew near. The coffin was empty.

"Are you satisfied now, friend John?" Van Helsing asked.

"I am satisfied that Lucy's body is not in the coffin, but that only proves that one thing."

"How do you account for it not being there?"

"Perhaps a body-snatcher," I suggested.

The professor sighed. "We must have more proof. Come with me." We left the tomb. Then he told me to watch at one side of the churchyard, while he would watch at the other. I took my place behind a tree.

I heard a distant clock strike midnight, and in time came one and two. I was chilled and unnerved. Suddenly, I thought I saw a white streak moving between two trees. A dark mass moved from the professor's side of the ground and hurried toward it. A little way off, a white, dim figure flitted in the direction of the tomb.

Going over to where I had first seen the white figure, I found the professor holding in his arms a tiny child. We took our way out of the churchyard. When we were some distance away, we struck a match and looked at the child's throat.

"We were just in time," said the professor. We decided that we would take the child to the Heath. At the edge of Hampstead Heath we heard a policeman's heavy tramp and laid the child on the pathway. We heard his exclamation of astonishment and then we went away silently.

I must try to get a few hours sleep. Van Helsing is to call for me at noon. He insists I shall go with him on another expedition.

September 27 - It was two o'clock before we found an opportunity. The funeral held at noon was all completed. Van Helsing walked over to Lucy's coffin and I followed. He again forced back the lead rim. A shock of surprise and dismay shot through me.

There lay Lucy, just as we had seen her the night before her funeral. If possible, she was more lovely than ever and I could not believe she was dead. The professor put over his hand and pulled back her lips to show the white teeth.

"See, they are even sharper than before." He touched one of the canine teeth. "She was bitten by a vampire when she was in a trance, sleep-walking. In trance she died and in trance she is UnDead, too. So I must kill her in her sleep."

This turned my blood cold. It began to dawn on me that I was accepting Van Helsing's theories. "How will you do this?"

"You return tonight to your asylum. I shall spend tonight in this churchyard. Tomorrow night you will come to me at the Berkeley Hotel at ten o'clock. I shall send for Arthur to come and also that fine young man of America. Later we shall all have work to do."

So we locked the tomb, got over the wall of the churchyard, and drove back to Piccadilly.

September 28 - We got into the churchyard over the low wall. The professor unlocked the tomb and entered first. He then lit a lantern and pointed to the coffin. Arthur stepped forward hesitantly.

Van Helsing said to me, "You were with me here yesterday. Was the body of Miss Lucy in that coffin?"

"It was."

Van Helsing forced back the lead rim and we all looked in. The coffin was empty!

"Wait with me outside and things much stranger are yet to be seen." He opened the door and we all filed out. Arthur stood silent.

Van Helsing took from his bag a mass of what looked like thin wafers. Next, he pulled out a mass of dough or putty. He crumbled the wafers up and worked it into the mass. Then he rolled the mass into thin strips and laid them in the space between the tomb door and its frame. I was puzzled at this and asked him what he was doing.

"I am closing the tomb so the UnDead may not enter."

"And is that stuff you have put there going to do it?" asked Quincey.

"It is."

"What is that you are using?" This time the question was by Arthur. Van Helsing lifted his hat as he answered.

"Communion wafers. I brought it from Amsterdam." There was a long spell of silence and then the professor pointed. Far down the avenue of trees we saw a white figure advance. It held something dark.

It was now near enough for us to see clearly in the moonlight. I could hear Arthur gasp as we recognized Lucy Westenra. The four of us made a line before the door of the tomb.

Van Helsing raised the lantern and we could see Lucy's lips crimson with fresh blood. When Lucy saw us, she drew back with an angry snarl.

Then she advanced to Arthur with outstretched arms. "Come to me, Arthur. Leave these others and come to me."

Arthur seemed under a spell and opened wide his arms. Lucy was leaping for them, when Van Helsing sprang forward. He held before her his little golden cross.

She jerked back from it and dashed past him to enter the tomb. She stopped as if she had met some invisible force. Never did I see such hate on a face. Van Helsing asked Arthur, "Am I to proceed with my work?"

"Do as you will, friend." Arthur threw himself on his knees and hid his face in his hands.

Van Helsing removed some of the sacred putty from around the door. We looked with horrified amazement as the woman passed through the space where a knife blade could barely fit. The Professor calmly restored the strings of putty to the edges of the door.

When this was done, he lifted the child from where it had been flung to the ground. We left the child in safety. Arthur and Quincey came home with me, and we tried to cheer each other on the way. We were all tired and slept, more or less.

Dr. Seward's Diary

September 29 - A little before twelve o'clock Arthur, Quincey, and I called for the professor. It was odd that we had all put on black clothes.

Van Helsing had with him a long leather bag, instead of his little black one. When he again lifted the lid of the coffin, we all saw that the body lay there.

Arthur said to Van Helsing, "Is it really Lucy's body or only a demon in her shape?"

"It is her body, and yet, not it. But wait a while and you shall see her as she was, and is."

Van Helsing began to take various contents from his bag, including his operating knives, a round wooden stake, and a heavy hammer. The stake was about three feet long with one end sharpened to a fine point.

All was ready. Van Helsing said, "It will be a blessed hand that strikes the blow to set her free. To this I am willing, but is there none among us who has a better right?"

Arthur stepped forward, though his face was as pale as snow. "Tell me what I am to do, and I shall not falter."

"Brave lad! Take this stake in your left hand and the hammer in your right. When we begin our prayers for the dead, strike in God's name. Then all may be well with the dead we love."

Arthur took the stake and hammer. Once his mind was set his hands never trembled. Van Helsing opened up his prayer book and began to read. Quincey and I followed as well as we could. Arthur placed the point over the heart. Then he struck with all his might.

The thing in the coffin twisted and hideous screeching came from the red lips. But Arthur never faltered. Finally, the body lay still. The hammer fell from Arthur's hand.

When we looked at the coffin again, a murmur of surprise ran through us. There was Lucy as we had seen her in life with her face of sweetness and purity.

Before we moved away from the tomb, Van Helsing said, "My friends, one step of our work is done. But there remains a greater task. We must find the author of all this sorrow and stamp him out. Shall you all help me?"

We each took his hand and the promise was made.

When we arrived at the Berkeley Hotel, Van Helsing found a telegram waiting for him.

"Am coming up by train. Jonathan at Whitby. Important news. - Mina Harker"

The Professor was delighted. "She must go to your house, John. Meet her at the station."

Over a cup of tea, Van Helsing told me of a diary kept by Jonathan Harker. He gave me a typewritten copy of it and also one of Mrs. Harker's diary at Whitby.

"Take these and study them well," he said.

Then I took my way to the station and arrived about fifteen minutes before the train came in. A sweet-faced, dainty-looking girl stepped up to me. "Dr. Seward, is it not?"

"And you are Mrs. Harker!" I answered at once. I got her luggage, which included a typewriter. In time we arrived. She knew that the place was a lunatic asylum, of course. I must be careful not to frighten her.

Mina Harker's Journal

September 29 - After I had tidied myself, I went down to Dr. Seward's study. At the door I thought I heard him talking to someone. To my surprise, he was quite alone. On the table opposite him was what I knew from descriptions to be a phonograph. I had never seen one and was much interested.

"I hope I did not keep you waiting," I said. "I heard you talking and thought there was someone with you."

He replied with a smile, "I was only entering my diary. I keep it in this." He laid his hand on the phonograph.

I blurted out, "Why, this is even better than shorthand! May I hear it say something?"

"Certainly," he replied. Then he paused and a troubled look came over his face. "The fact is I only keep a diary of my cases in it. It may be awkward. You see, I don't know how to pick out any particular part."

I said boldly, "Dr. Seward, you had better let me copy it out on my typewriter."

He grew deathly pale. "No! For all the world, I wouldn't let you know that terrible story."

"When you have read my diary and my husband's also, you will know me better. I must not expect you to trust me so far."

He certainly is a man of noble nature. Dear Lucy was right about him. He stood up and opened a large drawer. Several hollow cylinders of metal covered in wax lay inside.

"Take the cylinders and hear them. Then you will know me better. And I shall read over some of these documents." He carried the phonograph himself up to my sitting room and adjusted it for me. Now I shall learn something. . . .

Later - When the terrible story of Lucy's death and all that followed was done, I lay back in my chair. If I had not known Jonathan's experience in Transylvania, I could not have believed.

Dr. Seward's Diary

September 30 - Mr. Harker arrived at nine o'clock. If his journal be true, he is a man of great nerve. After reading his account I expected to meet a good specimen of manhood. I hardly expected the quiet, businesslike gentleman who came here today.

Later - It never struck me that the very next house might be the Count's hiding place! The bundle of letters relating to the purchase of the house were with the typed journals.

Jonathan Harker's Journal

September 29, in train to London - It is now my objective to trace that horrible cargo of the Count to its place in London. Later, we may be able to deal with it.

September 30 - Of one thing I am now satisfied. All the boxes that arrived from Varna were safely deposited in the old chapel of Carfax. There should be fifty of them there.

Mina Harker's Journal

September 30 - We met in Dr. Seward's office two hours after dinner. Professor Van Helsing sat at the head of the table with Jonathan and I on one side, and Lord Godalming, Dr. Seward, and Mr. Morris opposite us. The professor told us of the kind of enemy with which we are dealing.

After giving us a history of vampires, he went on. "When we find the dwelling place of this man-that-was, we can confine him to his coffin and destroy him."

While he was talking, Mr. Morris was looking steadily at the window. He got up quietly and went out of the room.

There was a little pause and then the professor went on. "It seems to me that our first step should be to discover whether all the boxes remain in the house. If any have been removed, we must trace —"

Outside the house came the sound of a pistol shot. The glass of the window was shattered with a bullet that struck the far wall of the room. I am afraid I am a coward at heart, for I shrieked.

We heard Mr. Morris's voice from outside. "Sorry! I fear I have alarmed you." A minute later he came in. "It was an idiotic thing for me to do. I apologize, Mrs. Harker. While the professor was talking there came a big bat, and it sat on the windowsill. I went out to have a shot."

"Did you hit it?" asked Dr. Van Helsing.

"I fancy not, for it flew away into the wood." He took his seat and the professor continued.

"We must trace each of these boxes. We must sterilize the earth in them so he can no more seek safety. Then we may find him in his form of a man between the hours of noon and sunset. We will battle him when he is most weak."

Mr. Morris said, "I vote we have a look at his house right now. Swift action on our part may save another victim."

They have now gone off to Carfax with the tools to get into the house.

Jonathan Harker's Journal

October 1 - I went with the party to the search with an easy mind. I never saw Mina so strong. Lord Godalming had slipped away for a few minutes but then returned. He held up a little silver whistle.

"That old place may be full of rats. If so, I have the fix," he said.

When we got to the porch of the house, the professor opened his bag and took out a lot of things. He sorted them into four little groups, one for each of us.

"My friends, we are going into a terrible danger and we need arms of many kinds. We must guard ourselves against his touch. Keep this near your heart," he said.

He lifted a small silver cross and held it out to me. He handed me a wreath of garlic blossoms to put around my neck.

"For other enemies, this revolver and knife. Friend John, where are the skeleton keys?" Dr. Seward tried a couple keys. He got one and the bolt shot back with a rusty clang. The professor was the first to move forward and step into the open door.

"Into Thy hands, O Lord," he said as he stepped over the threshold. The whole place was thick with dust. The professor turned to me, "You know this place, Jonathan. Which is the way to the chapel?"

So I led the way. After a few wrong turns I found myself before a low oak door with iron bands. We were prepared for some unpleasantness, but none of us expected such an odor! After pulling back on the first sickening whiff, we all set about our work.

A quick glance showed how many boxes remained. There were only twenty-nine out of fifty! A few minutes later I saw Morris step suddenly back from the corner he was examining. We all drew back. The whole place was filling with rats.

Lord Godalming rushed over to the great oak door and swung the door open. Taking his silver whistle from his pocket, he blew a low, shrill call. It was answered from behind Dr. Seward's house by the yelping of dogs. Three terriers came dashing round the corner of the house.

At the threshold, the dogs stopped and snarled. Lord Godalming lifted one and carried him in, placing him on the floor. He rushed at his natural enemies. The rats fled before him and the whole mass vanished. Bringing the dogs with us, we began our search of the house. We found nothing but dust.

The morning was coming in the east when we emerged from the front. We now know twenty-one boxes have been removed. We may be able to trace them all. I shall look up Thomas Snelling today.

October 1, evening - I found Thomas Snelling in his house, but he was not in a condition for remembering anything. I learned from his wife that he was only an assistant to Mr. Joseph Smollet. Smollet remembered all about the boxes. From a dog-eared notebook he gave me the addresses where the boxes were sent.

There were six in a cartload, which he took from Carfax to 197 Chicksand Street. Another six he left at Jamaica Lane. He also sent me to a Sam Bloxam, who told me he had made two journeys between Carfax and a house in Piccadilly. He had taken a total of nine boxes to Piccadilly. I went to Piccadilly and came across the house he had described. I was satisfied it was Dracula's next lair.

Dr. Seward's Diary

October 2 - The attendant came bursting into my room and told me patient Renfield had met with an accident. He heard him yell and found him lying on his face. I must go at once. . .

When I went to Renfield's room, it was obvious he had received some terrible injuries. I sent for Dr. Van Helsing. He was sinking fast and might die at any moment.

He opened his eyes and said, "I must say something before I die. He came up to the window in the mist. I wouldn't ask him to come in, though I knew he wanted me to. And then a red cloud seemed to close over my eyes. I found myself opening the window and saying, 'Come in!' I didn't mean for him to take any more of her life."

Van Helsing stood up. "He is here and we know his purpose. Let us arm ourselves. It may not be too late."

We hurried and with Arthur and Quincey took from our rooms the items we had used at the Count's house. Outside the Harkers' door, we paused. "This is life and death. Now!"

He turned the handle but the door did not yield. We threw ourselves against it and with a crash it burst open. On the bed beside the window Jonathan Harker lay with his face flushed, breathing heavily. Kneeling on the other side of the bed was his wife. Beside her stood a tall, thin man in black clothes. His right hand gripped her by the back of the neck.

As we burst into the room, the Count threw his victim back and sprang at us. But the professor was holding toward him an envelope filled with communion bread.

The Count suddenly stopped and shrank back. Farther he went back as we advanced with our crosses held out. The moonlight failed as a black cloud moved over it and Quincey lit a light.

When the light came on, we saw nothing but a vapor trailing under the door. Arthur and Quincey ran out of the room. Van Helsing woke Jonathan from his trance and we tried to calm both he and his wife.

The professor held up his cross. "You are safe for tonight, my dear, and we must take counsel together."

Art and Quincey returned to the room and the professor asked them to tell what they had seen.

Art answered, "I could not see him anywhere, but he had been to the study. The manuscript was burned and the cylinders of the phonograph were thrown on the fire."

I interrupted, "Thank God there is the other copy in the safe!"

Art went on, "I looked in Renfield's room but there was no trace of him. The poor fellow is dead, though."

Van Helsing turned to Quincey. "Friend Quincey, have you anything to tell?"

"I thought it good to know where the Count would go when he left the house. I did not see him. But I did see a bat rise from Renfield's window and flap westward. I expected to see him go back to Carfax, but he sought some other lair. The dawn is close and we must work tomorrow!"

Jonathan Harker's Journal

October 3 - It was finally agreed we should first destroy the Count's lair close at hand. We entered Carfax without trouble.

"And now, friends, we must sterilize this earth," said Van Helsing. He took from his bag a screwdriver and a wrench. The top of one of the boxes was soon thrown open.

Taking a piece of the sacred bread, he laid it reverently on the earth. Then he shut the lid and screwed it down. We aided him as he worked. One by one we treated each of the boxes in the same way.

I have written this on the train to Piccadilly.

Piccadilly, 12:30 - Just before we reached Fenchurch Street, Lord Godalming said to me,

"Quincey and I will find a locksmith. You go with Jack and the professor and wait in Green Park in sight of the house. When you see the door open, all of you come."

We took a cab to the park and sat down on a bench. We saw a four-wheeled coach drive up. Godalming and Morris got out. A working man with a basket of tools descended from the box. Godalming pointed out what he wanted done.

The man went to work. All at once the door swung open and he entered the hall with Godalming and Morris. When the locksmith had gone, the three of us crossed the street and knocked on the door. It was immediately answered by Morris.

The house smelled like the old place in Carfax. It was plain to us that the Count had been using the place freely. We explored the house. In the dining room we found eight boxes of earth. Only eight of the nine boxes we sought!

We opened the boxes and treated them as we did the others in Carfax chapel. Then we went in search of anything belonging to the Count. We found a little heap of keys of all sorts and sizes. Godalming and Morris took the keys and set out to destroy the boxes in the other houses. The rest of us are waiting for their return or the return of the Count.

Dr. Seward's Diary

October 3 - The time seemed terribly long while we were waiting for the coming of Godalming and Morris. We were talking together when we were startled by a knock at the door. It was the double knock of a telegraph boy. Van Helsing stepped to the door and opened it. The boy handed in a message.

Look out for D. He has just now, at 12:45, come from Carfax and hurries toward the south. Mina.

Van Helsing said, "The time is coming for action. Today this Vampire is limited to the powers of man and until sunset he cannot change.

We must hope Lord Arthur and Quincey arrive first."

About half an hour after we had received Mrs. Harker's telegram, there came a quiet knock at the hall door. Lord Godalming and Quincey Morris came quickly in and closed the door behind them.

"It is all right. We found both places. Six boxes in each and we destroyed them all," said Godalming.

"He will be here before long," said Van Helsing. "Hush! Be at your arms! Be ready!" We could all hear a key being softly inserted in the lock of the door.

Quincey Morris had always been the one to arrange the plan of action. With a swift glance around the room he placed us each in position. Dracula leaped into the room with a single bound.

Harker made a fierce cut at him with his great kukri knife. Only the evil quickness of the

Count saved him. The point cut the cloth of his coat. A bundle of banknotes and a stream of gold fell out.

I moved forward, holding the cross and communion bread in my left hand. I felt a mighty power fly along my arm. I saw the monster cringe back and blaze a look of baffled rage. With a dive he grabbed a fistful of money from the floor. He dashed across the room and threw himself out the window.

He tumbled onto the paved area below. We ran over to the window and saw him spring up from the ground. He turned and spoke to us. "My revenge is just begun! Time is on my side." With a sneer he disappeared through the stable door and away.

Sunset was not far off. We recognized that our game was up. The professor said, "Let us go back to Miss Mina. We can at least protect her. There is but one more earth box and we must find it. When that is done, all may yet be well."

Before the Harkers retired for sleep, the professor fixed up the room against the coming of the Vampire. He placed a bell nearby for them to sound in case of any emergency.

Quincey, Godalming, and I arranged that we should divide the night between us and watch over the poor lady. The first watch falls to Quincey.

Jonathan Harker's Journal

October 4, morning - During the night I was awakened by Mina. "Go, call the professor. I want to see him at once."

"Why?" I asked.

"I have an idea. He must hypnotize me before the dawn." Two or three minutes later Van Helsing was in the room. Mr. Morris and Lord Godalming were with Dr. Seward at the door.

"My dear Miss Mina, what am I to do for you?" he asked.

"I want you to hypnotize me. Do it before dawn. I feel that then I can speak freely." Without a word he motioned for her to sit up in bed.

He began to make passes with his hands in front of her, from the top of her head downward. Gradually, her eyes closed and she sat stock-still. The professor made a few more passes and then stopped. Mina opened her eyes but there was a faraway look in them.

"Where are you now?"

"I do not know. It is all strange to me!"

"What do you see?"

"I can see nothing. It is all dark."

"What do you hear?"

"The lapping of water. It is gurgling by. I can hear little waves on the outside."

"Then you are on a ship?"

"Oh, yes! I hear the sound of men stamping overhead as they run about. There is the creaking of a chain."

"What are you doing?"

"I am so still. It is like death!" The voice faded away and the open eyes closed again. By this time the sun had risen.

Mr. Morris and Lord Godalming started for the door, but the professor's calm voice called them back.

"Stay, my friends. That ship was at anchor while she spoke. There are many ships in your so great Port of London. Which of them do you seek?

We know now what was in the Count's mind when he grabbed the money. He has taken his last earthbox onboard a ship. He thinks to escape but we follow him!"

Mina asked, "Why need we seek him further? He has gone away from us."

"Because he can live for centuries and you are but mortal woman. Time is now to be dreaded since he put that mark upon your throat."

I was just in time to catch her as she fell forward in a faint.

Chapter 13

Dr. Seward's Diary

Dr. Seward's Phonograph Diary, Spoken by Van Helsing

This to Jonathan Harker. You are to stay with your dear Madam Mina. Our enemy has gone back to his castle in Transylvania. He is limited, though he is powerful. But we are all more strong together.

Take heart, husband of Madam Mina. In the end we shall win. As sure as God sits on high to watch over His children.

Dr. Seward's Diary

October 5 - At the beginning of our meeting, Mrs. Harker sent a message to say she would not join us yet. She thought it better for us to plan our movements.

Van Helsing put the facts before us. "The Czarina Catherine left the Thames yesterday morning. It will take her at least three weeks to reach Varna. In order to be quite safe, we must leave here on the seventeenth at latest. Of course, we shall all go armed."

Quincey added, "I understand the Count comes from a wolf country. I propose we add Winchesters to our weapons."

"Good!" said Van Helsing. "Quincey's head is level at all times but most so when there is a hunt."

Jonathan Harker's Journal

October 5, later - How strange it all is. As the evening drew on, Mina opened her eyes from sleep. She said, "Jonathan, I want you to promise me something on your word of honor."

"I promise."

"Promise me you will not tell me anything of the plans formed against the Count. Not one word while his influence remains on me."

I felt from that instant a door had been shut between us.

October 6, morning - Another surprise. Mina woke me early again and asked for Van Helsing. He came at once and asked if the others might come, too.

"It is not necessary," she said. "You can tell them. I must come with you on your journey." Dr. Van Helsing was as startled as I was.

"But why?"

"I am safer with you and you are safer, too. I know that when the Count wills me, I must go. I know if he wills that I come in secret, I must obey. You men are strong together and can stand against what would break down one who guarded alone. Besides, you can hypnotize me and perhaps learn something."

"Miss Mina, you are most wise. You shall with us come. I shall go make arrangement for the travel."

There was nothing further to say. I shall now settle all my business on earth and be ready for whatever may come.

October 15, Varna - We left the morning of the twelfth and got to Paris that same night. We took our places on the Orient Express. We traveled night and day, arriving here about five o'clock.

Mina is well and her color seems to be coming back. She sleeps a great deal but is alert before sunrise and sunset. It has become a habit for Van Helsing to hypnotize her at such times. It is evident that the Czarina Catherine is still at sea.

October 17 - Everything is fixed to welcome the Count on his return. Godalming told the shippers he thought the box sent aboard might contain something stolen from a friend of his. They are to alert him when the ship comes to harbor.

October 24 - A whole week of waiting. Mina's morning and evening hypnotic answer is unchanging. Lapping waves, rushing water, creaking masts.

Dr. Seward's Diary

October 27 - Most strange. No news yet of the ship we wait for. Just now Van Helsing told me he fears the Count is escaping us. He added, "I do not like that sluggishness of Madam Mina."

October 28 - A telegram arrived today announcing the ship's arrival in Galatz, not Varna. I think we all expected something strange to happen. Harker smiled a dark, bitter smile and put his hand on the hilt of his kukri knife.

"When does the next train leave for Galatz?" said Van Helsing.

"At six thirty tomorrow morning!" We all stared, for the answer came from Mrs. Harker.

"You forget that I am a train fiend."

"Wonderful woman," murmured the Professor. He stood up. "We shall follow him. And we shall not flinch."

CHAPTER 14

Dr. Seward's Diary

October 29 - This is written on the train from Varna to Galatz. When the usual time came, Mrs. Harker prepared herself for hypnosis. It took longer this time. At last her answer came.

"I can see nothing. We are still. There is a gleam of light. I can feel the air blowing upon me." She had risen from where she lay on the sofa. She raised both her hands with palms upward, as if lifting a heavy weight. And so it is that we are traveling toward Galatz in an agony of expectation.

Mina Harker's Journal

October 30, evening - The men are all so tired and worn out from their investigations. Professor Van Helsing got me the information

I have not yet seen. While they are resting, I shall go over it carefully. Perhaps I may arrive at some conclusion. . . .

I do believe I have made a discovery. Every minute is precious. My theory is this:

In London the Count decided to go back to his castle by water. It is the most safe and secret way. When the box was on land before sunrise or after sunset, he came out from his box. He met with a man named Skinsky to instruct him to arrange the carrying of the box up some river. When this was done, he murdered Skinsky to blot out his trail.

I have examined the map to find which river is most suitable. The Sereth is joined by the Bistritza, which runs up by Borgos Pass. The loop it makes is as close to Dracula's castle as can be.

Jonathan Harker's Journal

October 30, night - I am writing this in the light from the furnace door of the steamboat.

Lord Godalming is an experienced hand at this. He owned one on the Thames for years. We have no fear running at good speed up the river at night. There is plenty of water and the banks are far apart.

November 1 - Some of the Slovaks tell us that a big boat passed them. It was going at more than usual speed with a double crew.

Memorandum by Abraham Van Helsing

November 5 - Let me be accurate in everything. You may at first think that I am mad. We travel into more and more wild land. I began to fear the fatal spell of the place was upon Madam Mina.

We were near the top of a steep hill. On the summit of it was a castle, like Jonathan tells of in his diary. I took out the horses and led them to what shelter I could. Then I made a fire and made Madam Mina comfortable near it amid her rugs.

I drew a big ring round where Madam Mina sat. Over the ring I passed some of the communion wafers so that all was well guarded. Presently the horses began to scream till I quieted them. In the coldest hour the fire began to die and I was about to step forth to renew it.

It seemed as though the snow flurries and wreaths of mist took shape of women with trailing garments. Then they were before me in real flesh. They were the same three women Jonathan saw in the room. They twined their arms and pointed to Madam Mina.

"Come, sister. Come to us." Oh, the terror in her sweet eyes! My heart with gladness leaped. God be thanked she was not yet like them. We remained within the ring till the red of dawn began to fall through the gloom.

The horrid figures melted into the whirling snow and the wreaths moved away toward the castle. I turned to Madam Mina to hypnotize her, but she lay in a deep and sudden sleep. I have made my fire and seen the horses. They are all dead.

Jonathan Harker's Journal

November 4, evening - The accident to the steamboat has been a horrible thing for us. We have got horses and follow on the track. If only Morris and Seward were with us. We must only hope!

Memorandum by Abraham Van Helsing

November 5, afternoon - I am at least sane. When I left Madam Mina sleeping within the holy circle, I took my way to the castle. I found the old chapel. I knew that here my work lay. There was one tomb more lordly than all the rest. On it was but one word, DRACULA.

I laid in Dracula's empty tomb some of the wafer and banished him from it. Then I began my terrible task. Had it been but one, it would have been easier. But three! I can pity the poor souls now as I think of each in her calm, full sleep of death.

Mina Harker's Journal

November 6 - The professor and I took our way east from where Jonathan was coming. He found a hollow in a rock with an entrance like a doorway between two boulders. He brought in our furs and made a nest for me. Taking his fieldglass, he stood on top of the rock and searched the horizon.

"Madam Mina, look!" Straight in front of us and not far off came a group of men on horses, hurrying along. In the midst of them was a cart. On the cart was a great square chest.

"They are racing for the sunset. We may be too late." Then a sudden cry. "Look! Two horsemen follow fast, coming up from the south. It must be Quincey and John."

I took the glass and looked. Looking around I saw on the north side of the cart two other men. They were riding at breakneck speed.

One of them I knew was Jonathan. I got my revolver ready, for the howling of wolves grew louder and closer.

Closer and closer the different parties drew. Two voices shouted out, "Halt!" Lord Godalming, Jonathan, Dr. Seward, and Mr. Morris raised their Winchesters. Every man in the gypsy party drew what weapon he carried, knife or pistol.

Jonathan and Quincey forced their way to the cart from different sides. Nothing could stop them. Jonathan jumped upon the cart and with incredible strength flung the great box over the wheel to the ground. Mr. Morris had to use force to pass through the gypsies on his side. They cut at him with their knives and he defended with his great bowie knife.

I could see he was clutching at his side with his left hand. But he attacked one end of the box to pry off the lid, while Jonathan attacked the other. The top of the box was thrown back. The Count was deathly pale and the red eyes glared with a hateful look. The look changed to one of triumph as they saw the sinking sun.

But the sweep and flash of Jonathan's knife came through the throat. The same moment Mr. Morris's bowie knife plunged into the heart. Almost in a drawing of a breath, the whole body crumbled into dust.

The gypsies turned without a sound and rode away as if for their lives. The wolves withdrew and left us alone.

Mr. Morris had sunk to the ground. I flew to him, as the holy circle did not keep me back now. Jonathan knelt behind him and the wounded man laid back his head on his shoulder. He smiled at me.

"It was worth this to die! Look!" He pointed to me. The sun was now right down upon the mountaintop. The red gleams fell upon my face so it was bathed in rosy light.

"The curse has passed away!" And to our bitter grief the gallant gentleman died.

Jonathan Harker's Journal

Seven years ago we all went through the flames. It is an added joy to Mina and me that our boy's birthday is the same day as that on which Quincey Morris died.

His mother holds the belief that some of our brave friend's spirit has passed into him. We call him Quincey.

Godalming and Seward are both happily married.

I took the papers from the safe where they have been since our return so long ago. We could hardly ask anyone to accept these as proofs for so wild a story.

JONATHAN HARKER